The Boy,
the Rat,
and
the Butterfly

The Boy,
the Rat,
and
the Butterfly

Beatrice Schenk de Regniers

illustrated by
Haig and Regina Shekerjian

Atheneum 1971 New York

for
Francis

Three of them are going down the road. Peter
the Rat, Peter the Butterfly, and the boy called
Peter.

They don't seem to be going very far. And wherever they are going, they are not getting there very fast.

The boy called Peter is looking for treasure. And everytime he sees something that might be a treasure, he must stop and pick it up. He must look at it carefully to make sure it is a treasure worth keeping.

He has already found a large white stone as smooth as an egg, and shaped like one. And he has found almost half an egg shell. Blue. It must have been a bird's egg.

Sometimes he stoops to watch a parade of ants, sometimes just one ant carrying a seed or a scrap of dried grass. That takes a long time. Now he sees a white feather, so he picks it up and puts it in his pocket.

It is easy to see why the boy called Peter is not getting very far or going there very fast—not with all that stopping and stooping and looking for treasure.

As for Peter the Butterfly, it's a wonder he gets anywhere at all, the way he goes zigzagging across the road.

Zig left to taste the honey of a lacy white flower.

Zag right to a yellow flower that looks like a buttercup, and may very well be a buttercup.

Off he zigs left again to a purple clover. And oh—zag! There's another clover on the other side. Sweeter perhaps? No! No! Zig! Maybe he should stay with the first clo— well, zag—maybe— zigzag —zig—zag.

"I get dizzy watching that butterfly," says Peter the Rat. "If Peter the Butterfly would fly in a straight line, we might get farther faster."

But Peter the Butterfly keeps on zigzagging.

And, to tell the truth, Peter the Rat is not going very far very fast himself.

For one thing, he likes to talk, and he finds it hard to talk and walk at the same time. And even more than he likes talking, Peter the Rat likes to recite poetry. He walks a few steps, then something reminds him of a poem and he stops to recite it in a loud voice; with gestures.

Just now he looks up at the blue sky and is reminded of a poem. He stops to recite:

What is so rare as a day in June?
Then if ever come perfect days.
Then heaven tries earth if it be in tune
And over it softly her warm ear lays.

James Russell Lowell
Born February 22, 1819
Died August 12, 1891

On the lid of the box are some letters made of small sea shells. The letters make two words. The boy reads the words: T-R-E-A-S-U-R-E B-O-X

"I'm holding a treasure box," he tells Peter the Rat.

"Open it," says the rat.

"It's locked," the boy tells him.

"Unlock it," says the rat. "Turn the key."

"I'm afraid to," the boy says.

"Here, I'll do it," says the rat.

"No. I'll open it," the boy says.

Slowly he turns the strange key. The lid pops open.

"Well? What's inside?" asks the rat.

"Nothing much," says the boy called Peter. "A straw. It looks just like a drinking straw. But it has two words printed on it."

"What are the words? What are the words?" Peter the Rat comes closer.

"M-A-G—Oh. It says MAGIC STRAW."

Peter the Rat comes closer. "Anything else?"

"Yes," says the boy. "There is a piece of paper that says, hmmm, just a minute. D-I-R-E-C-T—it says DIRECTIONS. DIRECTIONS FOR USE."

"I'm very good at reading directions," says Peter the Rat. And he takes the paper right out of the boy's hand and begins to read the directions aloud. He reads with expression and gestures, as if he were reciting a poem:

DIRECTIONS FOR USE

USE THE MAGIC STRAW TO MAKE A WISH COME TRUE.
FOLLOW DIRECTIONS CAREFULLY.
ONE: ✳ DIP MAGIC STRAW INTO WISHING SOLUTION.

"Wishing solution? Is there some wishing solution in the treasure box?" asks Peter the Rat.

The boy looks in the box. "Well, there is a bottle. Yes! It's printed right on the bottle. W-I-S-H —WISHING SOLUTION. Do you want it?"

What is so rare as a day in June

The boy called Peter sees a leaf shape on the road and he stoops to pick it up. But it is only a leaf shadow. "This isn't June at all," he says. "It's August, I think."

"June. August. What does it matter?" says Peter the Rat. "It's a beautiful day." He stops and stretches one arm wide:

A thing of beauty is a joy forever.
Its loveliness increases. It will never

    John Keats
    Born October 31, 1795
    Died February 23, 1821

"It will never what?" asks the boy.

"I don't know," says Peter the Rat. "The page in the book was torn."

The boy stands up. He is sorry he can not put the leaf shadow in his pocket.

Peter the Butterfly zigs by. "A thing of beauty," he whispers. A moment later he zags past again whispering, "forever-ever-ever."

The boy and the rat watch the butterfly. His wings—yellow on one side—flash like sunlight as he flies. The other side of his wings is pale green with lines of darker green, and when Peter the Butterfly rests on a flower and folds his wings, he looks like a green leaf barely moving in the breeze.

"He *is* a thing of beauty," says the rat.

And the boy asks, "Will he be a joy forever? Will his loveliness increase? It will never...die?"

"Most butterflies," Peter the Rat explains, "have a very short life span. Once they turn from caterpillar to butterfly, they don't live very long. Our friend here, for example. His life span as a butterfly is about three days. We first met him Monday. Today is Wednesday. So I'm afraid his demise is imminent."

"He is so beautiful." The boy takes a deep breath. "I want him to live forever."

Peter the Butterfly perches for a moment on a milkweed stem. "Beauty. Joy. Forever-ever-ever," he says in his whispery voice.

Peter the Rat picks up the very stem the butterfly has perched on and, holding the milkweed with the butterfly in front of him, he stands in the middle of the road and recites:

The flower that smiles today
   Tomorrow—
Peter the Butterfly zigs off again.

       Dies.

Peter the Rat continues:

All that we wish to stay
   Tempts and then flies.
What is the world's delight?
   Lightning that mocks the night,
Brief even as bright.

   Percy Bysshe Shelley
   Born August 4, 1792
   Died July 8, 1822

The boy called Peter is not listening. He has found a winged maple seed. He has split the seed open and is trying to make it stick to the end of his nose.

"Look! Look at me!" he shouts.

Peter the Rat looks. There is the boy, his face turned up to the sky, a winged maple seed stuck on his nose, his arms straight out like wings, and he is spinning around and around and around and around until—*oof!* He stumbles and falls to the ground.

"Oh, help. Everything is spinning around," the boy says. "The sky and trees and grass are going around and around. And they are going a little bit up and down at the same time. . . .

"Oh, help," he tells Peter the Rat. "You're spinning around too. You and the sky and the trees and the grass."

"Don't be silly," says Peter the Rat. "I'm stand-
ing perfectly still. What are you holding in your
hands?"

Peter looks down at his hands. Everything has
stopped spinning. And sure enough! He is holding
something. A box. It is closed tightly and locked
with a key—a strange looking key.

"Not just yet." Peter the Rat looks at the paper again. "Let me read all the directions first."

TWO: ✳ BLOW THROUGH THE STRAW AND SILENTLY WISH YOUR WISH AS YOU BLOW.
THREE: ✳ A BUBBLE WILL BEGIN TO FORM. GO ON BLOWING AND WISHING. THE BUBBLE WILL GET LARGER AND YOU WILL SEE YOUR WISH TAKE SHAPE INSIDE THE BUBBLE.
FOUR: ✳ WHEN THE BUBBLE BURSTS, YOU WILL HAVE YOUR WISH.
FIVE: ✳ ONLY ONE WISH TO A CUSTOMER.

"Hmm." Peter the Rat looks at the directions again. "This may be dangerous. I think I'd better try it first. Would you please hand me that bottle of Wishing Solution?" He opens the bottle. He sniffs. "No smell at all. Now, if you will give me the Magic Straw…" Peter the Rat holds out his paw.

He puts the straw to his mouth and is about to blow through it. Then he stops and looks at the boy. "Now what do you think I'm going to wish for?"

"I don't know," the boy says.

"I know what you are thinking, " says Peter the Rat. "You are thinking that because I am a rat I will wish for cheese. Well, I'll show you—I can think of finer things than food."

"I think food is fine," the boy says.

"You may think I'm just a ratty old rat," says the rat.

"I think you're very nice," the boy says.

"I'm no ordinary rat." Peter the Rat stands with one foot on a stone and puts one paw on his chest. He looks as if he is getting ready to recite a poem.

"How many other rats do you know who recite poetry?" he asks.

"Not many," says the boy.

"Not *any!*" says the rat.

"That's true," the boy says. "You're the only rat I know."

"You'll see," says Peter the Rat. "I'm a rat of refinement. I have a delicate nature—delicate as a flower. I'm a very special—"

"Why don't you begin blowing through the Magic Straw and wishing your wish?" the boy asks him.

The rat dips the straw into the Wishing Solution. "Now," he thinks, "everyone will see what a rare and lovely creature I am. I am *not* going to wish for cheese. No."

And as Peter the Rat blows, a bubble begins to form.

The bubble grows big and bigger. "I have more than cheese on *my* mind," thinks the rat. And as he blows, the bubble takes on beautiful colors. The rat looks pleased and continues to blow.

The colors turn into flower shapes—deep blue violets and pale pink columbine, and the white flower called star of Bethlehem, and yellow mimosa blossoms—all inside the bubble.

A sweet smell comes from the bubble as more and more flowers take shape.

Peter the Rat keeps on blowing, and now the flowers in the bubble are taking the shape of a—

—rat. A rat made entirely of flowers.

"Now," thinks Peter the Rat, "everyone can see how beautiful I *really* am—all made of fragrant flowers." And he keeps on blowing.

As he blows, the flower-rat inside the bubble seems to be holding something very tiny between its flower-paws. Peter the Rat closes his eyes and blows. And whatever the flower-rat inside the bubble is holding gets bigger and bigger.

Soon, mixed with the smell of flowers, is another smell. Is it—can it be—the smell of cheese? Yes. The flower-rat inside the bubble is holding a piece of cheese, and the cheese is growing bigger and bigger and bigger. Soon there is no room for flowers in the bubble. There is only a huge ball of yellow cheese. The bubble bursts and Peter the Rat catches the cheese between his paws.

He sits down and begins at once to gnaw the cheese. "Mhhhmmm," he says with his mouth full, "flowers are fine, and so is poetry. But when you're hungry, there is nothing like a big smelly cheese."

Peter the Rat had dropped the Magic Straw when he caught the cheese. Now the boy called Peter picks up the straw. "I know just what I'll wish for," he says. "I will wish for the most wonderful treasure in the world. I'll wish for a—" Just then, Peter the Butterfly perches on the end of the straw.

"Oh go ahead," says the boy. "You can have your turn now if you want to. Go ahead and wish."

"Wish? What? Why?" The Butterfly flutters on the end of the straw.

"Wait," says the boy. "I'll dip the straw in the Wishing Solution and then you can blow your wish bubble."

"Bubble? Wish? Why wish?" the butterfly whispers.

"Go ahead and blow," says the boy. "I'll hold the straw for you."

And so, perhaps to please the boy, Peter the Butterfly begins to blow.

A bubble takes shape—as clear as glass. "Wish for *something!*" says the boy.

"Wish? Wish?" thinks the butterfly. "Why should I—what should I—wish?" And he keeps on blowing.

"You could wish to live forever," says the boy. "Peter the Rat told me your death is imminent. That means you will die very soon."

Peter the Butterfly likes the word *imminent*. It has such a pleasing sound, like the chime of bells far away. So he keeps blowing and thinking to himself as he blows, *"Imminent-imminent-imminent."*

The bubble grows bigger and bigger, clear as glass and no wish is inside. Nothing. Nothing at all.

"Imminent-imminent-imminent," says the butterfly to himself.

And suddenly the enormous bubble bursts with a small sound like the chime of bells far away. The butterfly falls to the road—dead.

His wings are folded and he looks like a pale
green leaf—or the pale shadow of a leaf—on the
dust of the road.

The boy called Peter stands very still. He stands very still and looks down at the butterfly. The boy stands so still he looks like a statue of a boy holding a magic straw in one hand and looking down at a dead butterfly.

Nothing moves. But from the boy's eyes tears fall—on the road, on the butterfly.

Peter the Rat comes close to the boy. He looks down at the butterfly.

"That's life," says the rat.

"But he's dead!" the boy cries.

"I know," says the rat. He recites the first line of a poem:

Tears, idle tears, I know not what they mean.

Now the boy begins to sob.

Peter the Rat does not go on with the poem.
He touches the boy gently with his paw. "Come
now," he tells the boy, "it's your turn. Remember?
You wanted to wish for some wonderful treasure."

The boy cannot stop sobbing.

"Here." Peter the Rat takes the Magic Straw. "Let me dip this in the Wishing Solution for you. ...Now. You can wish for a golden sea shell and when you hold it to your ear at night, in bed, you will hear all the lullabies of the world. Or maybe you will wish for a silver mirror and when you look in it you can see—"

The boy, who is not really listening, sobs more loudly.

"Now stop that!" the rat says. "Take the straw and begin to blow. You could even wish for some cheese if you can't think of anything better just now."

Without really listening or even thinking, the boy puts the straw to his mouth. He closes his eyes and blows. A bubble forms, small at first, and then bigger. It is perfectly round and about as big as a baseball.

As the boy blows, colors swirl through the bubble—colors of sky and grass and purple clover and—

"Look!" cries Peter the Rat.

Just as the boy opens his eyes to look, the bubble bursts—and zigzagging in front of him is a butterfly. Three butterflies. Their wings—yellow on one side and pale green on the other—flash like sunlight.

Now they are going down the road. The boy, the rat, and the butterflies.

They don't seem to be going very far. And wherever they are going, they are not getting there very fast.

And it doesn't matter, really.